Mrs. Ciafardoni

GASTON
The Green~Nosed Alligator

GASTON
The Green~Nosed Alligator

Written and Illustrated by
JAMES RICE

Illustrator of *Cajun Night Before Christmas*

PELICAN PUBLISHING COMPANY
Gretna 1994

ISBN: 0-88289-049-2

First printing, September 1974
Second printing, September 1976
Third printing, September 1982
Fourth printing, September 1989
Fifth printing, September 1994

Printed in Singapore

Published by Pelican Publishing Company, Inc.
1101 Monroe Street, Gretna, Louisiana 70053

GASTON
The Green~Nosed Alligator

If you were awake
        on last Christmas Eve,
The sight you beheld
        was hard to believe.

You saw old Santa,
        of that you were sure,
But not like you saw him
        in any previous year.

Hardly anyone saw,
        and very few know,
How it really began
        just one year ago.

Quaint old Santa Claus
    in his house made of ice,
Was working as hard
    as a barn full of mice,
Preparing for Christmas,
    the day of good cheer,
The day of all days
    he'd worked for all year.

Yet Santa seemed worried,
    his face didn't glow,
The reindeer were shirking
    and working too slow.

Their reasons were many,
        their excuses were old:
Prancer sprained his ankle
        and Donner caught a cold.

Vixen picked up a splinter
        and Dasher split his hoof,
They'd both crash-landed
        on top of a roof.

Cupid showed a stubborn streak
        and Dancer had arthritis,
Blitzen nursed a headache
        and Comet had psoriasis.

And most tragic of all
        another problem arose,
The light had gone out
        on poor Rudolph's nose.

The reindeer were not all
        that gave Santa distress,
The whole North Pole business
        was now in a mess.

With ice on his whiskers
        and frost on his breath,
An old man like Santa
        might shiver to death.

He searched the world over
        in less than a week,
To find the best spot
        to warm his cold feet.

In South Louisiana
        he found the right place,
With warm bayou waters
        and trees hung with lace.

Deep in the swamp
        called the Atchafalaya,
Where there's crawfish bisque
        and shrimp jambalaya,
Catfish from the river
        and friendly folks, too,
It was just right
        for starting anew.

He'd found a way station,
    the place that was best
To cover the Southland
    as well as the rest.

Old Santa and his elves
    picked a house on the bayou,
It was shaded with cypress
    almost hidden from view,
An old rambling structure
    with giant oaks around it
A great fireplace blazing
    and workshop well fit.

With tools and work tables
    for building of toys
Old Santa felt better
    in spite of the noise
That bounced from the walls
    and left his ears ringing—
With sawing and hammering
    and busy elves singing.

His reindeer had stayed
     at the North Pole alone,
Begging old Santa
     to please hurry home.

How could he finish
     his rounds in one night,
Without his nine reindeer
     to help in the flight?

The reindeer last Christmas
    had nearly run late,
Because of a rainstorm
    in this very state.

The cold, driving rain
    on that tropical breeze
Was worse than a hundred
    mad storm-tossed seas.

Snow was no problem,
    they'd fly through with ease,
But this kind of storm
    almost leveled the trees.

They'd found themselves grounded
    down in the dark bayou,
And poor Rudolph's red nose
    had lost its bright hue.

They'd bogged down and wallowed,
    not seeing their way,
No help had been Rudolph
    in thick gumbo clay.

Even then Santa's team
    had been in good health,
For a new mode of travel
    he'd give all his wealth.

Old Santa was worried
    and not at all sure
How he could accomplish
    his task as before.

The days were now fleeting,
    so little time remained,
It soon would be Christmas—
    the thought gave him pain.

He might have to postpone
    the day of good cheer,
Because of nine ailing
    and aging reindeer.

Santa poled down the bayou
    and let his thoughts roam.
The problem's solution
    he'd find near this home.

He poled through quiet pools
    under veils of soft lace,
Draped from tall cypress trees,
    it hung every place.

From out of the corner
    of his left eye he spied
In the tree tops a sight
    that all logic defied.

He tilted his head
    and looked up above
To see an alligator
    take off like a dove.

For there flew ol' Gaston
    as sure as you please,
Swooping and gliding
    through the tops of the trees.

"Sacre! Look at Gaston,
    something sure is not right,
"He flies like a bird!
    Twice as fast! What a flight!"

While ol' Gaston flew
    he put on a show,
The envy of the gators
    he left down below.

While most of the alligators
    swam muddy and slimy,
Ol' Gaston flew high
    and kept clean, almost shiny.

"Stop, you strange creature,
    and come here to me!"
Shouted old Santa,
    exploding with glee.

His problem was solved,
    no more reindeer he'd need.
Ol' Gaston would help,
    there was no need to plead.

He'd train seven others
    to fly with a skiff,
Full of toys and goodies
    and every good gift.

Again and again
    the gators would try
To follow ol' Gaston
    and learn how to fly.

But they'd crash into trees
    and fall on their tails,
They'd try it again
    and still they would fail.

But they wouldn't give up
    'till they'd mastered the skill,
Of gliding through treetops
    with never a spill.

Now practice was over,
    it was near time to leave,
For in a few hours
    'twould be Christmas Eve.

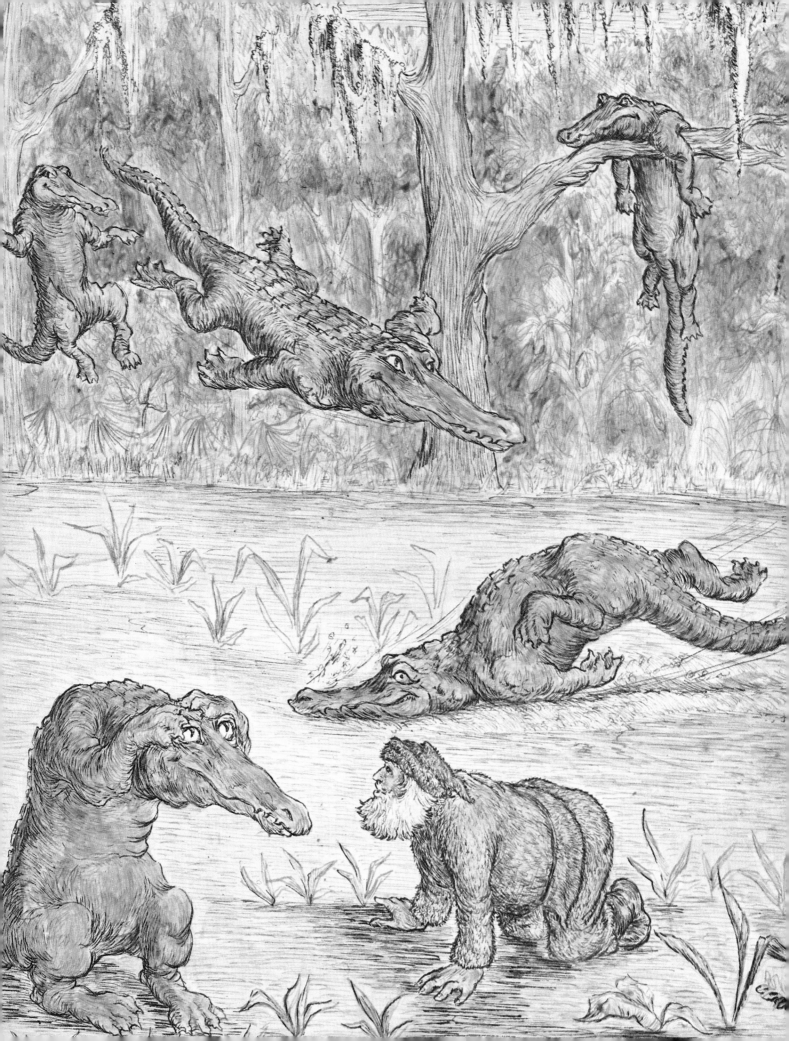

They loaded the gift bags
    in the skiff up so high,
Then hitched up the gators
    and got ready to fly.

The gators lined up
    all ready to go,
They'd have to move fast,
    no time to go slow.

"Hey, Gaston! Hey, Tiboy!
    Hey, Pierre and Alceé!
"Gee, Ninette! Gee, Suzette!
    Celeste and Reneé!

"Come on, you alligators,
    let's be on our way,
"We have to be through
    before the new day!"

They didn't miss a stop
     on their fantastic flight,
New records for speed
     were the standard that night.

And back on the bayou
     at just before dawn,
A sleepy old Cajun
     looked up with a yawn,
To see in the shadows
     an impossible scene—

A little old man
     with an outlandish team
Slipping past his view
     like a quick flash of light,
With a wave of his hand
     and an echo so slight.

And a voice saying clearly
before he vanished in tow,
"MERRY CHRISTMAS TO ALL
'TILL I SAW YA SOME MO'!"